For Nina with love – AB

For David – AW

First published in 1999 by Macmillan Children's Books
a division of Macmillan Publishers Limited
25 Eccleston Place, London SW1W 9NF
and Basingstoke
Associated companies worldwide

First U.S. Edition 2000

ISBN 0-316-93910-2
[LOC # to come]

10 9 8 7 6 5 4 3 2 1

Printed in Belgium

Over in the
Grasslands

Anna Wilson and Alison Bartlett

Little, Brown and Company

Boston   New York   London

Over in the grasslands . . .

Over in the grasslands
in the heat of the sun
Lived an old mother rhino
and her little rhino one.
"Munch," said the mother.
"We munch," said the one.
So they munched all day
in the heat of the sun.

Over in the grasslands
where the lakes are blue
Lived an old mother hippo
and her little hippos two.
"Swim," said the mother.
"We swim," said the two.
So they swam all day
where the lakes are blue.

3

Over in the grasslands
in a nest in a tree
Lived an old mother eagle
and her little eaglets three.
"Squawk!" said the mother.
"We squawk!" said the three.
So they squawked all day
in their nest in a tree.

Over in the grasslands
with a stretch and a roar
Lay a family of lions
and their little cubs four.
"Play," said the mother.
"We play," said the four.
So they played all day
and they roared and roared.

5

Over in the grasslands
in their big beehive
Lived an old mother bee
and her little bees five.
"Buzz," said the mother.
"We buzz," said the five.
So they buzzed all day
in their big beehive.

Over in the grasslands
playing all sorts of tricks
Lived an old mother warthog
and her little warthogs six.
"Oink," said the mother.
"We oink," said the six.
So they oinked all day
playing all sorts of tricks.

Over in the grasslands
in the grass long and even
Lived an old mother hare
and her little hares seven.
"Nibble," said the mother.
"We nibble," said the seven.
So they nibbled all day
in the grass long and even.

Over in the grasslands
where the sun shines late
Lived an old mother toad
and her little toads eight.
"Hop," said the mother.
"We hop," said the eight.
So they hopped and they hopped
while the sun shone late.

Over in the grasslands
in the hot sunshine
Lived an old mother jackal
and her little jackals nine.
"Run," said the mother.
"We run," said the nine.
So they all ran around
in the hot sunshine.

10

Over in the grasslands
in a big warm den
Lived a family of monkeys
and their little monkeys ten.
"Sleep," said the grown-ups.
"We sleep," said the ten.
So they slept all night
in the big warm den.

One

Two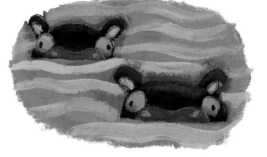

Three

Four

Five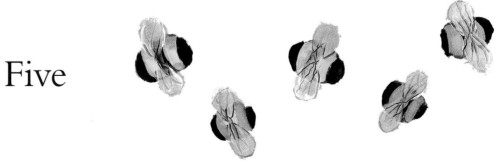

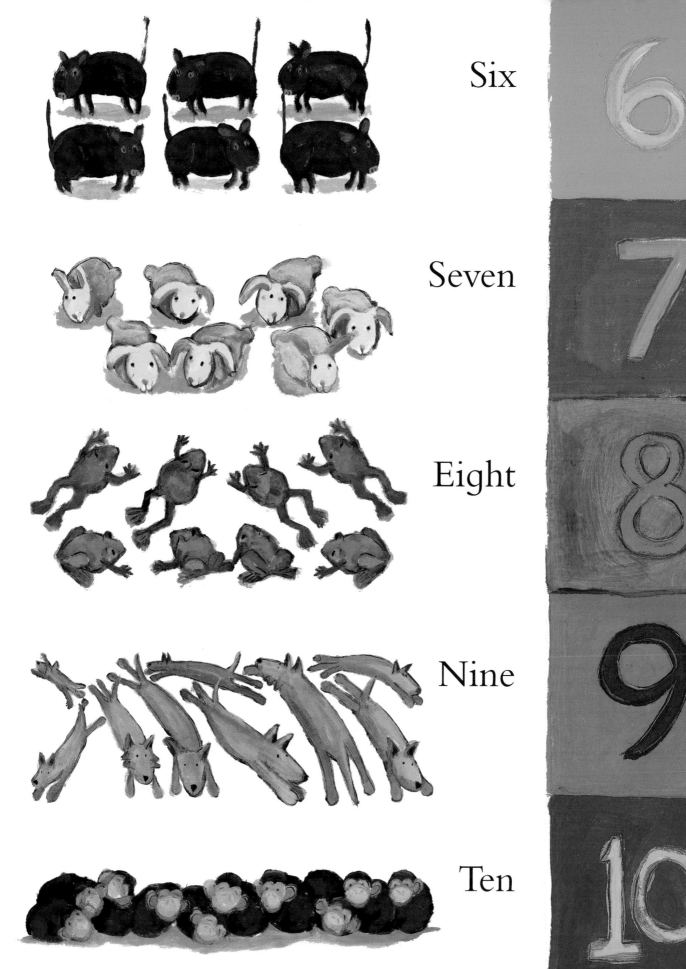

Six

Seven

Eight

Nine

Ten